Death at Jamestown

by Tracy Wainwright

TLC Wainwright Publishing, LLC
VIRGINIA

Death at Jamestown

A Historic Triangle Mini Cozy Mystery

Cover design by Tracy Wainwright

Contents

CHAPTER 1

SUZANNE had seen enough. She'd taken more than a dozen pictures on her phone. The proof was at her fingertips. Mr. Lowell might be a devoted dad, but an injured employee he was not. No man with a severe back injury would be carrying his three-year-old on his shoulders. She scrolled through the pictures. Nor would he have given his 6-year-old a bouncy piggyback ride. There were a couple times he grimaced, but his pain obviously wasn't bad enough for him to be out of work still.

She didn't like turning this kind of report into her contracting agency. The bums claiming disability while downing booze in front of the TV all day in between golf games and nights out at the bar she never had a hesitation about. There was satisfaction in saving a company from supporting a lowlife making a fraudulent claim. There wasn't much pleasure in turning in a dad who actually used his time for his family. Still, she wasn't the one who'd lied on a workman's comp form.

A bang reverberated throughout the historic park and she jumped. Her eyes flew across the dirt to the portly man demonstrating seventeenth century firearms. After the third blast since she'd arrived that afternoon, her body shouldn't react, but it did.

She turned and smiled. If she could, she'd thank Mr. Lowell for choosing Jamestown for his outing. She hadn't been there in years, since bringing her nieces when they were young. She shook her head. Bethany would be graduating high school in a month. Unbelievable. Brittany had just gotten her learner's permit. The girls were growing up into young ladies before her eyes. She never believed older people when they talked about how fast kids grew up, but it did seem like last week when she was playing with her nieces the way Mr. Lowell played with his children.

Suzanne slipped her phone in her pocket and strolled to the path leading to the exit.

A piercing scream halted her steps. She turned. A mom, arms wrapped around a boy of about ten, backed out of a small building. Her eyes wide. Even from thirty feet away, Suzanne could tell she was shaking. Several employees in period garb rushed to her.

"There..." She swallowed. "There's a man in there. On the ground. I think he's been shot. Blood. There's so much blood."

A young woman in a long dress and cap stepped forward, ducking her head in the doorway. "Oh my gosh. She's right." She pulled a cellphone out of an unseen pocket and tapped away.

Hopefully she was calling 911 and not posting on social media.

Suzanne shook her head. The girl was young, but that didn't give her the right to assume she would hit the net before calling for help.

"Yes, I'm calling from Jamestown Settlement. There's a man. It looks like he's been shot."

Suzanne scanned the gathering crowd. There were between forty and fifty people in the settlement replica area. A group of older tourists with matching lanyards. Three or four families with small children. Two teenagers looking much less bored than when she'd seen them trailing behind one of the families in the ships area.

No one seemed to be taking too much interest. No one appeared to be attempting to avoid looking interested.

She checked her watch. Three forty-two. If she calculated correctly, the gun demonstration began on each hour and half hour and lasted about seven or eight minutes. If someone shot this man and timed it with the fake gun blast, they'd have had five minutes to leave the area. Plenty of time to nonchalantly walk out of the log houses, through the museum building, and get in a car.

Just in case, though, she pulled her phone back out. Holding it about waste level, she took a series of photos. She first took an overview, then some close-ups. Next, she switched to video and let her phone capture the crowd's reactions in real time. Three minutes of video should be adequate.

Several other patrons also had their phones out, but she doubted their reasoning was the same as hers. Everyone seemed to want to be part of the latest news stories, as long as they weren't the victim. She speculated that at least a dozen photos would be running viral by the end of the hour, breaking the news before the first reporter made it on scene.

Sirens pierced the air. If she was going to get any closer and capture more details than she had, she'd have to act fast. People huddled in groups around the house in question. Two employees stayed with the mother and young boy who'd made the gruesome discovery. She wouldn't risk asking her questions before police arrived, but she logged the woman's face in her memory in case she wanted to follow up.

She slipped around the crowd to the house. It wasn't

her case, wasn't her problem. She wouldn't get a check from investigating this man's death, but it was in her blood. A P.I. couldn't turn off their curiosity, or their compulsive desire to know the truth.

At the doorway, she paused and glanced in. A man in khakis and a navy short sleeve shirt lay face down on the dirt floor. His salt and pepper hair was caked with blood. A pool of the life-sustaining liquid lay beside him. A piece of paper stuck out of his left back pocket. What she assumed was his wallet created a bulge in his right one. His phone was in his right outstretched hand. His left must have been captured underneath of him.

Holding her phone low, she tapped the button to take several pictures. Grateful she'd upgraded to the latest model a few weeks ago since the lighting was lacking. Clouds must have covered the sun in the last few minutes while she was taking stock of the scene.

"Whatcha doin,' Suzanne?"

She turned and grinned. "Just taking a peek, Tony. Haven't touched a thing."

He matched her upturned lips. "Except the camera on your phone."

She glanced at her hand and brought the accused device to eye level. "All turned off."

He rolled his eyes. "It takes half a second to hit the power button. I might not be a high-paid private investigator, but I am a detective with almost as much experience as years you've walked this earth."

"I might have taken a picture or two."

"You know we're going to ask for a copy of them."

She nodded. "I'd expect nothing less."

Tony turned his head. "Cumming, you can come document the scene. Juniper and Harris, you start interviewing the crowd. I'm going to question Mrs. Marsh and see what she observed." His gaze met hers. "Let's give my officers some space, huh?"

She stepped backward. "Of course." She glanced behind her. "Why don't we go sit on that bench. I've been walking all afternoon."

He held out a hand indicating for her to lead the way.

She sat, her gaze gravitating to the scene.

"On a case?"

"First of all, I've been widowed for eight years and am perfectly okay with the dropping of the 'Mrs.'"

He dipped his head.

"Second, of course. Know me to wander around tourist attractions for the fun of it?"

"No, I suppose not. Ever since the girls got too big to be excited about a place they've been to a dozen times before. How're Brianna, Brendan and the girls, anyway?"

"Good. Crazy busy as always. The girls are ready for school to be over. I think they're both working this summer. Brendan works too much, and Brianna loves her job."

"So, same as always?"

She nodded. Tony was a good friend, but a better detective. He hadn't forgotten why they sat on a bench in the middle of an olde town. Perhaps he had forgotten, however, that she couldn't be distracted from her mission by small talk. "Ask your questions, Tony. I know you have at least a billion."

He grinned, his eyes wrinkling at the corners. "At least. First is the obvious, see anything unusual today?"

CHAPTER 2

SUZANNE reviewed her afternoon. Following Mr. Lowell to the park. Staying far enough away he didn't feel stalked. Documenting his activities. Enjoying the normalcy of other families enjoying a beautiful spring afternoon at one of the area's most attended historically accurate replicas. After going through the day in her head, she answered. "No, not really. Stuck just close enough to my subject to get what I needed and not be noticed."

"How about right before the body was discovered?"

"I was on my way out." She described where she was and what she observed. She glanced to her left.

"There's something else."

"It's not anything I saw or heard, really. Just a suspicion."

"Your conjectures are often right on."

Suzanne met his gaze and held it, silently acknowledging the compliment. "I checked my phone right after the woman screamed. My best guess is the firing of the rifle during the weapons demonstration was a handful of minutes before then."

"How many is a handful?"

At this point most detectives would be furiously taking notes, but Tony's ability to remember details of an interview rivaled her observation skills. Near perfect. "Seven or eight, as best I calculated. You can confirm that with the re-enactor. He'd know exactly what time he shot the gun off."

"First," he said copying her tone from earlier in their conversation, "they're not re-enactors. They're interpreters. Second, he may not know the exact minute, but close enough to give a timeframe to work with. Thanks."

She grinned. "I know and you're welcome." She stood. "So, if there's nothing else, I do have another job to do today, and a report to write up."

He held out his right hand, palm up. "You know that's not all."

She sighed. "You don't trust me to get the pictures to you? I'll email them to you tonight."

"Of course, I trust you, Suzanne. I also know that you might be inclined to not send me 'unimportant' photos and investigate them yourself."

"I'm stunned at such an accusation, Tony. I have a full-time job that keeps me busy enough not to need to stick my nose in a police investigation."

"I'm sure you're about to collapse from shock. Still, I'll take your phone for a minute, if you don't mind."

"You know I don't have to give it to you."

"I also know that getting a warrant is a hassle and how much my officers give you in the way of support when you need it. I'd hate for that relationship to dry up like the Sahara."

She knew it was an idle threat, kind of. Only because he knew she wouldn't resist his request. He also knew she wouldn't give it to him freely. She slipped her phone out of her back pocket and handed it to him.

He glanced down at the locked screen and raised an eyebrow at her. "It's locked."

She leaned over. "Huh. So it is."

"What do you want, Suzanne?"

"Nothing that would compromise the case, but if there's something that comes up you think I can help with, you share with me."

"You drive a hard bargain woman."

"It's part of the job description."

"More like singed on your DNA," he mumbled.

She smirked and reached over and pressed her thumb

on the home button. Her phone lit up.

He scrolled through her most recent pictures and shook his head. "Of course you took a video of the crowd. And pictures of everyone who was present right after the body was found."

"I'm sure others did, too. See how many people had their phones out?"

He squinted and groaned. "I wonder how many of those are being shared online as we speak."

"All of them?"

He groaned again. "At least I can count on you not to blast your pictures all over social media."

"True."

He scrolled past the last, or first if she took chronology into account, picture of Mr. Lowell and his children to one of Brittany holding up her learner's permit. "Guess that's all of them. I counted. I expect fifty-three pictures and one video in my inbox before nine tonight."

"Of course."

He handed her phone back. "Brittany's driving now, huh?"

"Yeah. She's doing really well. Much better than Bethany did."

He laughed. "I thought that girl was going to lose her license the first year she had it she got so many tickets."

"Me, too. She's learned to slow down and pay

attention to road signs. No tickets in six months."

"Good." He stood. "Thanks, Suzanne. If you think of anything else, or discover anything as you pour over those photos, call me."

"Absolutely."

He held her gaze for several heartbeats. "Thanks in advance, so you feel guilty if you hold anything back from me. You're a good investigator, but you don't carry a weapon. Neither do you have backup if you get in a tight spot."

"I have backup."

"Right. How is Bart?"

Blood rushed to her cheeks. "He's good. Sammy and Christina giving him a run for his money."

"I imagine his detective skills come in handy with teenagers."

Especially ones whose mother was a narcissist. "That's an understatement."

"It's good he has you. What Candy did to him could have really messed him up."

"First," they were back to this again, "he doesn't *have* me. We're friends, we work in the same business. Second, she did really mess him up." And, unfortunately, his kids. She was off enjoying the high life with her new boyfriend in Miami while Bart was left to clean up a financial mess and keep his kids out of the system.

Tony chuckled. "There's a pool at the station, you know."

She narrowed her eyes. "What kind of pool?"

"Two actually. One guessing when y'all will officially announce you're an item."

"The other?" She knew he didn't forget to explain that one, but was tormenting her.

"When y'all will get married."

"Humph. Who said I'll ever get married again?"

"Seventy-two out of seventy-three JCC officers."

"I don't suppose you're the one dissenter?" she asked.

"Nope. Peter. But he's a skeptic about everything romantic."

"I always knew I liked that boy."

Tony didn't answer. He glanced across the grounds.

"Guess you have an investigation to continue."

"Yep. Thanks, again Suzanne. I'm glad you were here."

"I'm sure it wasn't by accident."

"You know how I feel about coincidences."

"They don't exist," they said in unison.

There wasn't anything else for Suzanne to do or catalog at the park, so she once again strode toward the exit.

In front of the entrance, several emergency vehicles took up the driveway closest to the building that held the gift shop and museum. Some first responders pushed a gurney covered with a sheet toward the ambulance. She picked up her pace.

CHAPTER 3

SUZANNE arrived next to the square box of a vehicle as the doors were swung open. "Brendan, hey."

Her brother-in-law looked up and smiled. "Hey, Suzanne. Fancy seeing you at a crime scene."

She held her hands up, palms out. "I was here working another case, I promise. Just happened to be in the right place at the right time."

"Unlike Tr–this guy."

"You know who it is," she exclaimed.

"Williamsburg's not that big."

"We are at a tourist spot, Brendan. It could have been an out-of-towner."

"Could have."

"But it's not."

He stared at her. "You know I can't give you information."

"He's dead. It's not like you're violating his healthcare rights."

"Still..." he turned to help Jack lift the rolling bed into the awaiting transport. As he slid it forward, the sheet caught on something and pulled down.

Suzanne gasped. "Tristan Jenkins." What was Williamsburg's most well-known lawyer doing at Jamestown? And who would want him dead?

Brendan glared at Jack and yanked the cover back up. They slid the gurney in the rest of the way and slammed the doors.

"Suzanne..."

She met Brendan's eyes. "You didn't say a word. Got it. You know I won't cause you any trouble."

"I know, but..."

"I might cause myself trouble. I've already gotten that lecture from Tony."

"Good." He rounded the ambulance to the driver's door.

She followed. "See you tomorrow night at Mom's?"

"Like Brianna would let me miss our monthly family dinner."

"It should be weekly."

"Says the woman with no kids who writes her own schedule."

The words weren't meant to slice through her, but the

jab to her gut hurt just the same.

"Sorry, Suzanne. I didn't mean–" He ran his fingers through his hair. "I'm an idiot."

"No, you're not. You're a hardworking guy with a hardworking wife and two great, crazy, busy kids. I know you and Brianna can't change when you work, I just miss you and the girls." The closest thing she had to her own children.

"Still...anyway, yes, we'll be there. With dessert and our calendars in hand. Maybe we can squeeze in another dinner before Bethany's graduation."

"That'd be great. See you then, Brendan."

He saluted her and hopped up in his seat.

Suzanne scanned the parking lot after the ambulance pulled out and down the road. A few police cars sat scattered around, but the fire trucks had long gone. She turned back toward the building. A couple of the families she'd seen in the fort exited the building. What a day it must have been for them. The poor mom and boy who'd discovered Tristan would probably need counseling.

Seeing there was nothing else she could do or glean from the area, she headed to her car. Before pulling out and heading to her next job, she shot off a text message to Bart.

Tristan Jenkins shot execution style at Jamestown.

Her phone buzzed as she turned on the settlement's

namesake road. She resisted checking it and continued to drive to her next client's house. He claimed to have severe whiplash after being rear-ended while delivering pizzas. The accident was more verifiable than the injury.

She pulled next to the curb across from the house listed on her file. A rental car sat in the driveway, so he was home. The front window was uncovered and she could see someone sitting on the couch. A glance through her binoculars and a double check of her file confirmed it was the man in question. He didn't look like he'd be moving anytime soon.

She picked up her phone. Bart's text glared at her. *What!?! Call me.*

"Hey," he picked up on the first ring. "What in the world? Tristan Jenkins is really dead?"

"Yeah, I was there on a job when the body was discovered." She reviewed the last hour while keeping her eyes fixed on the house across the street.

"Wow. I don't suppose there's any idea who could have done it."

"I certainly don't have anyone in mind. Tristan's a good man." Suzanne sighed. "Was a good man. Lenora's going to be devastated. I bet Tony goes to tell her himself."

"Man, I mean we see those living under the law bite it all the time, but someone like Tristan."

"I know. You don't suppose he had something shady going on. He knows the law inside and out and would know how to get around it."

"No way. I've known Tristan my whole life. He's good people. If he had something underhanded going on, I'd pay you my next commission."

"I'd take you up on that, but I'm not willing to put up my check on that bet. The odds would be one in a million," she replied.

"You got that right."

The man inside the house rose from the sofa and stepped out of the room.

"Suzanne?" Bart asked after several quiet moments.

"Yeah?"

"You good?"

"Yep. Just watching my latest client."

"Anything interesting?"

The man returned to his living room with what looked like a soda can. She grabbed her binoculars. Yep. "No. This one might be legit, but it'll take a few more days to know for sure."

"Good. You could use a quiet evening after the day you had." He paused. "What about your other case?"

She pursed her lips and dropped her extra eyes on the seat beside her. "Guy's fine. He was out hanging with his kids."

21

"Thus the visit to Jamestown."

"Yeah."

"You're going to investigate Tristan's murder, aren't you?"

"I wouldn't say that," she hedged.

"But?"

"I did take a lot of pictures today. It won't hurt for me to look at them all a little closer."

He didn't reply.

"You got a job going on?" she asked after a long moment of silence.

"Of course I do. Have you ever known me not to be working?"

She grinned. "No."

"Then don't try such a lame question to redirect me."

She laughed. "Who says I was trying to redirect? The whole conversation's been about my day. Wanted to know what you have going on."

"Not anything exciting. Why don't I come by and look through those pictures with you. Four eyes are always better than two."

Suzanne shook off Tony's words from earlier in the day as they pushed their way forward. She and Bart were friends, cohorts bouncing ideas off each other for work. Nothing more. He saw things differently than she did. They made a good team. "Sure," she finally answered. "I should be home by eight."

"Perfect. I'll bring Chinese?"

"See you then."

CHAPTER 4

THE DOORBELL rang as Suzanne pulled the last photo off her printer. She tossed the stack of pictures on her coffee table as she sauntered to the door. She turned the locks and pulled it open. The aroma of soy sauce, sweet and sour sauce, and eggrolls greeted her. "Hey."

"I thought we might be up late, There's a case of Dr. Peppers in the plastic bag."

"You know how to speak my language." She closed the door behind him.

Minutes later, she plopped on the opposite end of the couch, overflowing plate in one hand and soda in the other. "I put the rest in the fridge." She set her drink down and inhaled. "This smells divine. I've only had a protein bar since an early lunch."

"You never eat well."

She shrugged as she shoveled in the first forkful of fried

rice and dripping meat.

"Okay, maybe never isn't the right term."

She chuckled.

They stayed on small talk while eating. Suzanne could multi-task in many situations, but when she dug into a collection of evidence looking for clues that would rather stay hidden, she liked to have all her senses working together.

She set her empty plate on the table next to her and drained the last few drops of her drink. "You about ready to dig in?"

Bart popped the final bite of his eggroll in his mouth, wiped his hands on a napkin, and nodded.

She picked up the thicker stack of photos. "We'll start with these. I started taking snapshots a minute or two after the body was found."

"What's the other stack?"

"The ones I took of my client. We'll only look at those if necessary."

"You think there was something or someone you might have missed?"

"I saw what I was looking for. Someone really out of place I might have noticed, but if the killer were at the park before the murder, he might have tried to blend in," she answered.

"I agree." He stroked his stubbly chin. "I'm guessing

you don't remember seeing Tristan before he was discovered."

She shook her head. "No. I'd have remembered that. There wasn't anyone there I knew."

"Okay. Why don't you get a notebook. We'll catalog the pictures and who's in them."

"You and your notebooks." She stood to retrieve one from her desk. She grabbed a yellow legal pad and blue gel pen and handed them to him when she returned. "You know I'll just be typing these up on the computer later."

"I know. There's something about writing things out by hand, though. Plus, if you type the notes up, you have a chance to look at them a second time." He examined the writing utensil. "You and your gel pens."

"If I'm going to write something, I want it to look pretty."

He shook his head and tsked.

"Let's just get started. These are the first ones I took."

They examined each picture, numbered them, and catalogued who was in each one. Who stood by who, and what kind of look they had on their face.

She turned the last photo from the first stack over and stood. Stretching, she glanced at Bart. He was as much of a bulldog as she was when it came to a mystery. Most of the P.I. work they took required very little investigative work and held even less mystery. "Want to call it a night or want another Pepper?"

Bart checked his watch. "Only quarter to eleven. I don't have an early job in the morning. How about you?"

"Nope. Not needed until lunchtime."

"Then caffeine-infused sugar water it is."

Suzanne grabbed one for each of them and had the first nose-tingling sip swallowed before handing Bart his. "Nothing looks obvious."

"I agree." He motioned to the remaining stack. "Shall we tackle those? I'll pretend I can't figure out who your target is."

"Even though we both know you'll have him pegged by the second photo."

He grinned. "Only because of your stellar investigative skills."

She rolled her eyes. "Don't try flattery on me now. It's meaningless when I know it's sarcastic."

He met her gaze. "You know I think you're an amazing detective."

Heat rushed to her cheeks. "Now you're just...I don't know what you are, but cut it out. We have at least another hour of work to do."

His smile widened, deepening his dimples. That she did not notice. Nor did she occasionally dream about.

"Okie dokey."

She raised her eyebrows. "Seriously?"

He laughed and handed her the notebook. "Your turn to record. I'm going to have carpal tunnel if I don't take a break."

She took the notepad and pen as he picked up the top remaining picture. On the next to last picture, her hand halted above the pad. "Let me see that."

He handed her the photo and leaned in.

She pointed to the back of a man with black jeans, grey shirt, and black baseball cap. "I haven't seen him in any other pictures."

"Me either." He squinted and bent closer, then moved back a tad. "I guess it would have been too much to ask that he'd have been looking at the camera."

She pursed her lips, holding back a smirk.

He met her eye. "What?"

"Need me to get a magnifying glass, old man? Then you won't have to work so hard at finding the right distance to see the picture clearly."

"Ha, ha. I'm not that much older than you and my eyes work just fine, thank you."

She lost the battle against her smile. "Goodness, I don't know. You're in a whole other decade. The mid-life one."

"Whatever, whippersnapper. We'll see if you're still laughing in six years."

"Oh, I will be."

He raised his eyebrows.

"By then, you'll practically be fifty."

"Older *and* wiser, don't you forget it."

"You're going to have to prove that one." She nudged him with her shoulder.

"Want to bet on this case? First one to solve it gets bragging rights for a whole year."

"And takes the other out to eat at the Boathouse."

He stuck his hand out. "You're on."

She shook his hand and refocused on the picture. "Slim build."

"Can't see much hair, but I'd say sandy blond with a bit of curl."

She pulled it closer. "I agree. Why don't I go blow it up and make us each a copy? I need to email Tony anyway."

"You haven't sent him these already?"

"I have." She stood. "But I'll let him know that we found this extra guy."

"Don't think his amazing detective skills will figure it out all on their own?"

"Just keeping my word," she threw over her shoulder as she entered her office.

She sat at her desk and pulled up the picture in question in a photo editing program. After cropping and enlarging it, she printed two highest quality copies. Today's technology really came in handy. She never worked when pictures had to be sent off or a P.I. had to own their own dark room, but she could imagine the challenges taking so much time for such a simple thing caused. Of course, criminals also had the same advances at their fingertips, making it easier for them, too.

However, it often came down to something basic. Few of the people she came into contact with in her line of work were as smart as they thought they were. And she'd worked enough cases with Tony to know the same was accurate about most criminals.

She handed Bart his copy. "Here you go."

"Thanks." He set it on the table, stood, grabbing his dinner and drink trash. He peaked into one of the containers as he strode to the kitchen. "Guess I know what you're having for breakfast."

"Beef and broccoli. Breakfast of champions."

"And private investigators who stay up too late."

"Who live alone," she added.

"There is something about 'party of one' that's unmotivating to cook."

"Agreed. Truth is I never had a great desire to cook, though." She followed him into the kitchen and tossed her paper plate, two empty bottles, and takeout container in the garbage. "I didn't even ask what Sammy and Christina were doing tonight. You didn't need to be home to do dinner with them?"

"Nah. Sammy was working after school today and Christina went home with a friend to work on a yearend project. My mom agreed to get them home, fed, and in bed before midnight." He walked back to the living room.

"She's a good lady."

"Yes, she is. I'd be a wreck if I didn't have her."

Suzanne looked at him. His dark hair was disheveled, his shirt was wrinkled with a grease stain from dinner, and his socks didn't match. "I can imagine."

He grinned. "You like me a mess. You wouldn't know what to do with me if my clothes were pristine and every hair was in place."

"You're right, I–"

He studied her. "What?"

"Just something you said," she mumbled as she riffled through the stack of photos on the table. She snatched up one of Tristan.

He moved closer, looking over her shoulder. "Whatcha thinking?"

"This." She tapped the back pocket. "This piece of paper. I wonder what it was."

"Hmm. Not like Tristan Jenkins to have anything out of

place. I get what you mean. It's almost as if he'd just stuffed it in his pocket."

"I agree. Wonder what the chances of Tony telling me what was on that paper are?"

Bart shrugged. "Tony's a good guy. Your chances are much better if they have a hard time figuring out how it fits."

"True," she said while stifling a yawn. She lost the battle.

"All right. Enough sleuthing for one night." He kissed her forehead. "Get thee to bed and we'll talk on the morrow."

She rolled her eyes. "I've definitely kept you up too late. You're talking in your native, early days tongue."

"She's such a comedian." He unbolted the door. "Sleep well, my friend."

"You, too." Suzanne ignored the scattered photos call to be straightened up and headed down the hall to her bedroom. The bed beckoned her, but she pushed through her getting ready to shut down routine before accepting the invitation.

She shot off an email to Tony, plugged her phone up and climbed into the cool covers.

CHAPTER 5

SUZANNE had an hour to spare before she needed to be anywhere. She drove by the Jenkins house. Several cars filled the driveway and spilled out onto the road. Lenora had plenty of support. They were members of one of the largest churches in Williamsburg, so she'd probably have more food than she could eat for weeks.

What was it about people overloading the grieving with meals when so many people found it difficult to eat while grief was raw? She guessed they just wanted to do something, and cooking was a tangible thing that felt like helping. And there was the fact that the house of the grieving would be overflowing with extra people in those initial days. She guessed it really did make sense. But not being a cook, that was never her first thought.

She passed the house and turned around in a neighbor's driveway. She pulled up to the closest empty spot and debated going in. Suzanne knew who the couple were, but hadn't ever had a direct interaction with them beyond an introduction at some fundraising function.

She was sure Tony had asked Lenora as many questions as he dared in her shock. Chances were she wouldn't know anything anyway. Who would? Tristan's death made no sense. Bart was right about him. He was an upstanding guy.

He wasn't a criminal lawyer, so didn't come in contact with the dregs of life. As far as anyone knew, he'd been faithful to Lenora for thirty-five years and had great relationships with their two children. Their grandchildren visited each summer. She remembered seeing lots of snapshots posted online of what they called 'grandcamp.'

Tristan worked hard. She'd never heard even the faintest hint of discord between his partners or complaint from employees among the gossips of Williamsburg. He went to church and volunteered in the community. It made no sense.

She put the car in gear. She would offer her condolences another day. Certainly she wasn't going to question Lenora at that moment. What she could do, though, was run by his office.

She pulled into the law firm's parking lot fifteen

minutes later. She didn't have much time, but it was worth checking out. Who did she know there?

Tanner. A paralegal who was friends with Monique. She grinned. It paid to have a young next-door neighbor with connections to people she wouldn't normally come into contact with.

A secretary with red, swollen eyes forced a smile as Suzanne walked through the front door. "Good morning, may I help you?"

"Hi, I know it's a hard day around here, but was wondering if Tanner would have a few minutes."

"Tanner Monroe?"

Suzanne didn't know his last name, but there couldn't be more than one Tanner in a small law firm, surely. She nodded.

The secretary, her name plate designated her as Deborah Zuno, tapped on her phone. "Tanner, there's someone here to see you." She paused. "I...I'm not sure." She met Suzanne's gaze.

"Suzanne Marsh."

Deborah repeated her name and hit a button on her phone. "He'll be right here."

"Thank you."

Suzanne turned and walked to the waiting area with a handful of chairs and small table covered in financial and family magazines. Her phone buzzed.

She pulled it out. A text from her mom. She could answer that later. The time read eleven twenty-three. She had a half hour still.

"Suzanne."

She looked up, slipped her phone back in her pocket, and offered her hand. "Morning, Tanner. Good to see you."

He shook her hand. "Thanks." He raised his right eyebrow. "I'll admit I'm curious about your visit. I can only guess it has something to do with Tristan's death."

"You always were an astute young man."

He laughed. "I'm not that much younger than you."

She grinned. "Good genes. I'm really older than you think."

"Shall we go to a meeting room? I passed an empty one on my way down."

"Sure. Thanks." She followed him down a hallway and into a glass-encased office.

"What can I help you with?" he asked as he sat.

"I'm sure the police have been by this morning already."

He confirmed with a head nod. "They wanted Tristan's files, but haven't gotten a warrant yet."

"Yeah, his death doesn't really make any sense. The only thing that seems even remotely possible is if there's some disgruntled client."

38

"That still doesn't compute. Tristan's clients all loved him. They knew he'd do everything he could to help them make decisions in their best interest. He would forego a bigger fee for more hours by convincing clients to take a simpler route. He never charged for phone consultations that lasted less than half an hour. He was more than fair with everyone. He was generous."

"That's the impression I got." She stared off into space. "So, no idea who he might have been meeting at Jamestown or why there?"

"No. Not that I can think of."

"Do you know his cases well?"

He nodded. "Most of them. I do a lot of typing and research for a lot of contracts. He's a stickler for detail."

"Any case you can think of that might make someone upset? Maybe not the client, but a family member? People get testy when it comes to estates and losing what they believe is rightfully theirs."

He shrugged. "Can't think of..."

She leaned forward, holding the question on the tip of her tongue.

"There's one case he insisted on working alone. He does–did that once in a while."

"Know what case it was?"

"No. He kept it quiet. There were just some more cases of closed-door phone calls and off site meetings in the last week or so."

"Tristan keep a calendar?"

Tanner grinned. "Yeah. An old-fashioned one on his desk."

"Any chance I can see it?"

"I don't think that'd hurt. Nothing out in the open like that has the expectation of confidentiality, right?"

"Right." She stood. "Now work?"

"Sure." He led her to Tristan's office, a large, impeccably kept space. His desk was what she had envisioned – a massive hard wood structure with a glass top. There was a computer on one side and a handful of framed pictures on the other. His calendar lay in the middle. She walked around it. "He kept all his appointments here?"

"Yes. Deborah keeps all the partners schedules on the digital corporate calendar, but Tristan liked to have his written down and easy to access. Deborah comes, um came by every evening before leaving to make sure neither of them missed any appointments."

"She fill in some for him sometimes?"

"Yes."

"Thus the two different handwritings."

He leaned and turned his head. "Huh. It is pretty obvious."

She pointed to three separate entries over the last ten

days labeled 'CV.' "You know who these are?"

"No, but I can look into his files."

"Thanks. He had Jamestown two thirty written down on yesterday. Strange place for a meeting."

"Sure is. But Tristan always bent over backwards for clients. He'd meet them wherever they were comfortable. At a coffee shop, in their home. One time he held a two-hour meeting in the waiting room of a medical clinic while his client's wife received chemo."

"Okay. That helps it make a little more sense, but Jamestown is still an odd place to have a legal meeting."

"You'd be amazed the things people request."

"I shouldn't be." Her phone buzzed again, reminding her she had limited time. "So, this CV might be the case Tristan was working on in private. I'd appreciate if you could text me anything you find out." She grabbed the small notebook and pen she kept in her left back pocket and scribbled her number. "Guess we don't really know if yesterday's meeting was tied to those initials or not, but it's just as good a place to start as any."

Tanner didn't respond.

She wove around the desk to the door. "Thanks, Tanner. I know today's a hard day around here."

"No problem. Anything I can do to help find out who did this to Tristan. He really was the best boss around here." His ears turned red. "Not that the other partners aren't nice, just..."

"I understand. Men like Tristan Jenkins don't come along every day."

He nodded.

She checked her phone as she walked down the hall. A thank you text from Tony. He must have finally read her emails.

CHAPTER 6

SUZANNE bit into her burrito and caught a string of cheese attempting to soil her shirt. Her day had left her too much time to ponder. She'd thought of every person she could with the initials CV. None of them made sense to her and she had no way of knowing if they were a client of Tristan's or not.

She took another picture of the man she was investigating doing nothing. This guy was either really injured or just a bum without a life beyond his couch. At this point, she'd buy either theory. Her phone vibrated in her hand. An unknown number. The message made it clear who it was from.

Found three names: Claudia Vaughan, Clay Vickerman, Clinton Vines

She shot off a reply. *Thanks, Tanner! Any chance I could know what Tristan was working on for them?*

He sent her a twisted lips emoji. Guess not. She was overstepping just asking. Time to call Tony.

"Detective Henderson."

"Hey, Tony. I know you have my number in your contacts. Don't get all official with me."

"Afternoon, Suzanne. Are you calling to gain information or give it?"

"A little of both." She hoped. Tony was an astute detective. He may already have garnered the information she had.

"All right. I'll bite. What do you have for me?"

"First," she began with their regular banter, "there was a slip of paper sticking out of Tristan's back pocket. Any chance you'd tell me what was on it?"

"A very small chance. Share with me what you have, first."

"I went by Jenkins, Harmon, and Dexter this morning."

"Must not have been too early since I missed you. Of course, looking at the time stamp on the email you sent me, you had a late night last night."

"Not too bad."

"Bart keep you company?"

She was not going to answer that question. "I spoke with Tanner Monroe. He agrees with everyone I've talked to that Tristan was an upstanding, squeaky-clean guy."

"Who else have you talked to?" The mirth in his tone

44

hinted that he was still harassing her about Bart.

"A few people. Anyway, I got a glimpse of Tristan's schedule."

"Yeah, we had Deborah print out the last year."

"Did you look at the calendar on his desk?"

"I was interviewing employees, not gathering physical information," he answered. "I'd assume someone cataloged a photo of it."

Good. She had something that might take him and his team who knew how long to get to as they combed through the information they collected. "There were three appointments with a time and initials instead of a last name. They also had no location, like most of his appointments."

"You don't think these were in the Itinerary Deborah keeps for the lawyers?"

"Not sure. I didn't see that one."

Shuffling of paperwork came over the line. She waited. And waited.

"Here it is. You say all three appointments were recent?"

"Last two weeks."

"What dates?"

Suzanne closed her eyes and pictured the desk calendar. "The seventh, tenth, and fifteenth."

"There are a few appointments on those dates, but

45

none that match. What were the initials?"

"CV."

"Nothing."

She knew that already. Well, assumed, at least, that those appointments wouldn't be on the master schedule.

"We have all the information we collected this morning to go through and are still trying to convince a judge to give us a warrant. Harding is insisting he needs reason to think Tristan's murder was connected to a client before giving us access to all his files. He'd be much more likely to give one file than all of them. Any chance you know who those initials belong to?"

"I got a few options. Three to be exact."

"Care to share?" Tony asked.

Suzanne checked her subject through her binoculars again. Nothing. "What was on the sheet of paper?"

"You do realize I could call Tanner Monroe and get the information from him?"

"What fun would that be? Come on, you know I never get in the way or cross any lines. I'm the one who called you, remember?"

"Because you're stuck and want something in trade."

She didn't reply. No need acknowledging what they both knew to be true.

"KV," he finally responded.

"Another set of initials. Interesting. A relative of the client, maybe? V isn't a very popular initial."

"That seems like a reasonable guess."

"Deduction, my dear Tony. I never guess."

He chuckled. "All right, I gave you what I have, now your turn."

"Claudia Vaughan, Clay Vickerman, and Clinton Vines."

"Great." He paused. "That helps. We'll work on the judge for a warrant for just those three files."

"When you get them, don't forget to look into if any of them have a relative with the first initial K."

"Goes without saying. Thanks Suzanne."

"Anytime, Tony. I'm sure we'll talk again soon."

CHAPTER 7

BUZZING broke into Suzanne's dream about having dinner with Mark. He looked healthy and young and was full of laughter. Eight years and it still sometimes hit her like an F5 tornado.

She reached over at the incessant noise. "What?"

"Good morning, sunshine."

She glanced at her bedside clock. Barely after eight. "I don't work regular hours, Tony. Had family dinner last night. I like sleep."

"Because I work nine to five, right. If you don't want what I have…"

She rubbed her eyes. "You know I do."

"We have the gun."

"What?" She sat up.

"I know you heard me, so I won't repeat myself. There was a robbery at a convenience store on one forty-three last night and we caught the guy. Weapon he used was a twenty-two, just like Tristan was shot with. Thought we'd test it."

"It came back a match."

"Sure did."

"Think it's the same guy?"

"Nah," he answered. "Hair doesn't match and this guy's built more solid. Claims a buddy gave it to him in exchange for some weed."

"A gun for grass? That's a pricy high. Sounds like someone was anxious to get rid of it."

"My thoughts exactly."

"So whatcha need?"

"Can't I call just to share info with you?"

She shook her head and grinned. Not a chance. "Nope. I mean you could, but you wouldn't."

"Guy's not talking. He doesn't remember what his pal looks like. Could be white, could be black, could be Hispanic. Could be tall, but he also might be short. Could be fat or average. He can't bring himself to remember."

"You need me to dig?"

"I almost hate to ask, but it's not like you're unfamiliar with the areas these guys run in. They'll not utter a syllable to my guys. You know how they clam up as soon as they see a uniform. You still have some contacts?"

"Always," she stated.

"I'll give you where we picked this guy up and the home address he gave us. Maybe you can dig around, see if you can get a source of the gun."

"It'd be my pleasure." She grabbed her notebook and pen from the bedside table. "Go ahead."

He rattled off the information.

"Stay safe. Don't put yourself in unnecessary danger."

"Yes, father."

"Humph. If I was your father—"

"you'd listen to me a whole lot better," she finished with him.

"All right, Ms. Smarty. Now that you're awake you can get to work like the rest of the world."

After hanging up, Suzanne started her coffee pot, then began her wakeup ritual with a hot shower. As she sipped on her liquid kick starter, she typed a message to Bart. *Heading to East River.*

Her toast popped up and she tossed it on a plate. She'd slathered one slice with peanut butter and was halfway through covering the other with strawberry spread when her phone vibrated.

"Morning."

"Why is it you're going to East River? Don't tell me Tristan had client there. Or you do."

She relayed her earlier conversation with Tony.

"Good thing I have a slow day."

"No way. They'll smell cop on you from a mile away."

"I'm not a cop," his voice came across hard.

She sighed. "No, but you carry yourself like one. Your formal training in criminal justice sends off vibes to the criminal element. Not a soul will talk to me, not even the ones who know me, if you come."

"Fine. But check in every ten minutes, no five."

"Bart..." Why was it all the men in her life treated her like she was ignorant or helpless?

"I know you can take care of yourself, but no one is invincible. Not even you. Not that you care, but others do."

She let his comment slide. She did not have a death wish. She and God weren't on good enough terms since Mark's death for her to be certain she'd go where he was when her time came.

"Just agree to keep me updated. And take your mace."

"I always have that with me. And my steal pipe is under my seat."

"Good. So, if you don't want me to go, why'd you call?"

"Found out what was in Tristan's pocket."

"You had new information to barter with, I'm guessing."

"Good guess." She filled him in on the day before and

her call from Tony.

"He'd love to have you on staff."

"Nah, I can work beyond perimeters he has to stay in. Works better this way."

"No thoughts on the initials?"

"None I've come up with. I didn't know any of the clients Tanner shared with me. Except maybe Claudia Vaughan, I think she's been in the paper for some philanthropy things."

"Yeah, I've come across her and her husband Richard a time or two."

"Well, his initials don't match the second set," she said.

"No. Between you and Tony and his minions, you'll figure it out."

"Is it wrong I want to be first?"

He laughed. "I don't know about wrong, but I'm not shocked."

"I wouldn't think so. You have played a hand or two of cards with me."

"One day you'll learn to play for fun and not just to win."

"Maybe."

"I'm feeling more and more behind. My current case is keeping me too busy to do my own investigating into Tristan's death. Looks like the odds are in your favor for receiving that dinner."

"I won't complain."

"I'm sure. How about we take another stab at cards tonight?"

She had no legitimate excuse not to. Still, Tony's words from the other day stuck like a splinter under her nail. Just because the whole police department thought she and Bart should be dating, didn't make it so. Or change their friendship.

"Still there?"

"Yeah. Tonight sounds good. I'll order the pizza."

CHAPTER 8

THE BELL rang when Suzanne walked through the door of the convenience store. She wandered to the refrigerated section on the back walk and grabbed a bottle of her favorite bubbly, syrupy drink. In the aisle walking toward the counter, she snatched a bag of cheddar popcorn. She plopped both on the counter. "Hey, Mike."

"Well, well, if it isn't Ms. Suzanne. Been too long sweetheart." He scanned her items. "Four thirty-six."

She handed him a five. "I know. Work keeps me busy, haven't had a chance to get down here lately."

Several coins dropped into the tray on the customer side of the cash register. She plucked them up and tossed them in the small jar next to it.

"What brings you around now?" He grinned. "Miss me?"

"Of course. How's your mom doing?"

"Her heart's not so good, but she's still plugging along."

"I'm sure you're looking out for her, making sure she takes her medication."

"Whenever we can afford it."

Suzanne needed to come east more often. It was easy to get isolated in her own world and forget there were people who worked hard and still struggled to afford life-giving medicine. "I know she's grateful to have you."

"I'm sure glad I still have her. And now Janice will be able to help more since she'll be living with us?"

"Yeah?"

His grin widened. "Making an honest woman of her next month."

"That's great, Mike. Congrats."

The door opened and a ding acknowledged a new customer. Suzanne glanced at the guys in matching shirts and grimy jeans. The tall one dipped his head. The other rambled on about a crabby supervisor.

She turned back toward Mike. "I do have a question for you."

"No doubt."

She smiled. "Police pulled a gun off a perp yesterday who robbed your competition down the street. Any idea about him?"

"Yeah, I know the kid. Drug dealing thug. Low man thinks he's big."

She nodded, but didn't reply.

"Kid goes by Slinger. Grew up around here. No one knows who his dad is. His mom's been strung out since before he was born. Guess he didn't have a real chance."

"Slinger. Thanks. Know who he hangs with?"

"Now, Ms. Suzanne, you ain't goin' around them people. You're cute and all. They don't respect a nice woman like you."

She held up her keys. "Got my mace in hand at all times and my friendly steel pipe is in my car. I can take care of myself."

He looked over her shoulder and she glanced back. The two construction workers stepped up beside her. She moved to the end of the counter and waited for them to finish their transaction. Once they exited she leaned over. "Help me out, Mike. I'm assisting on a murder case. Good, upstanding guy everyone loved and respected was gunned down two days ago. That pistol Slinger had matched the bullet. So unless you know where he got the gun, I need a resource who might."

He stroked his goatee. "You know I help whenever I can."

"I know that."

"You promise you'll keep your eyes open, don't even give them a second to think you're vulnerable?"

She drew an X over her chest with her right pointer finger. "Promise."

"All right. Slinger lives in the Waterways apartments. There's another kid there, trying to keep his nose clean but his big brother runs with Slinger. His name is Dom. Apartment seven C."

She reached over and squeezed his hand. "Thanks, Mike. You're invaluable to me."

"Just care about my community. Would love all these drug pushers gone."

"I know. One step at a time." She stopped at the door and turned. "I'll see you within the next month with the best wedding present ever."

"You don't–"

She stepped through the door and cut him off. Five minutes later she drove into the Waterways apartment complex. A few people loitered around. Their eyes followed her as she pulled into an empty space. She grabbed her pipe and stepped out of the car. Adrenaline spiked in her blood and fueled her to hold her head high and stride across the parking lot as if she owned the place.

She met the eyes of three men sprawled out in front of

a doorway a couple apartments down, then turned her gaze back on the numbers. She raced up a set of steps labeled with the number seven. On the third floor, she located apartment c. She knocked.

"What," a male voice demanded from the other side.

"Dom, I'm Suzanne. Mike at the store sent me."

The door cracked open, the chain still in place. A young, black face peaked out. She guessed him to be about Bethany's age. Since he wasn't in school, he must be a year or two older.

"Hi."

"What do you want?"

"I'm working a murder case. Gun was used in a robbery yesterday by a guy called Slinger. Trying to find out where he got the gun. Mike said you might be able to help."

He eyed her down and back up. "You five-o?

"No, P.I."

He glanced down again. "Pipe was smart."

She dipped her head.

"Slinger was bragging about the deal he made last night. Some rich kid traded it for a bag of grass. Idiot. He could have gotten ten bags for that."

"Know the name of this idiot rich kid?"

"Nah. Don't nobody go by real names around here."

"You do."

He shrugged.

"He have a nickname?"

"Princy."

"Yeah?"

"Yeah, his real name is something royal and he thinks he's all high and mighty because he lives in that uppity plantation neighborhood. People 'round here don't care long as he keeps brining his cash."

"Know what he looks like?"

He shrugged. "Skinny, white kid. Probably a couple inches shorter than Slinger."

"Thanks, Dom. You've been really helpful."

He started to close the door and she stopped it with her foot. She pulled a business card out of her pocket and slipped it through the crack in the doorway. "You ever need anything, ring me. I'd be glad to help you out."

He eyed the small piece of paper.

"It's a real offer."

"Cool."

She turned and the door clicked behind her. Now to get back to her car and out of the neighborhood intact.

CHAPTER 9

"RUMMY." Bart set down the last of his cards face up.

Suzanne resisted the urge to groan. Her card luck must have gone to bed early that night. She gathered the cards and shuffled them.

"Princy, huh?"

"Yeah. Any thoughts?"

He picked up the cards she dealt in front of him. "Think his name is William or Harry or something?"

"Could be." She organized her hand.

"Maybe it's more literal. Like he's actually named Prince."

"Or King."

"Someone would actually name their child King?" he asked.

She shrugged. "You've seen the crazy names people have."

"True."

"Why don't we go do a search, see what options there might be."

He glanced at his hand and smirked. "Sure you want to quit now? I'm about to win again."

She eyed her cards. "Might as well."

He followed her to her office. She woke up her computer. "All right, let's try royal names."

A collection of website suggestions appeared. She clicked on one. "Nope. Just various names that mean royal. Not what we're looking for."

"It is possible."

She looked up at him. "These barely educated drug addicts are going to know that Ryan means little king?"

"Okay, maybe not."

"How about names that actually include 'king'?" She typed her new search parameters in and chose a website. "King. It is there."

"Who'd have thought?" He leaned in over her shoulder. "There's also Kingman, Kingsbury, Kingsley, Kingston, and Kingswell."

She grabbed a scrap sheet of paper and scribbled the names down, then typed in her search bar again. "There's Prince, Princeton, and Prinze. Not too many options."

"Eight possible names."

"Five."

He raised his eyebrows.

"Remember the paper in Tristan's pocket? It had the initials KV on them. Bet there's a connection."

"You're a smart cookie." He grinned. "I'm guessing there's no chance you could get access to the files of the client names you passed on to Tony."

"No way. He'd never let me see those."

She headed to the kitchen and grabbed a glass. "You want a drink?" she hollered.

"Sure."

"I'm getting water."

"That's fine."

She filled two glasses from the dispenser on the refrigerator and handed him one when she returned to the office. "How about we cross reference the K names with those on the ones we got from Tanner?"

"Good idea." He typed away on the computer.

After several searches and draining her glass, Suzanne strolled to the kitchen and came back with a bowl of peanuts. She offered them and Bart paused his online exploration to grab a handful.

"A bit tedious, huh?"

He glanced back at her. "At least it's more active than spying on someone watching TV all day."

"True that."

She set the bowl on the corner of the desk and stepped back. She folded herself into the cushioned rocking chair she often read in.

"Well, look at that."

She popped up and looked over his shoulder. "What?"

"There's a police banner for one Kingston Vines a little over a year ago. Possession and DUI."

"Clinton Vines son, you think?"

"It would fit. He was in his fifties. Son is, well was nineteen when he was arrested."

She checked her watch. "It's only eight-thirty. Too late to pay the Vines a visit? Only they would know if there's a possible connection between their son and Tristan."

He closed the internet windows and stood. "Not too late, unless we let grass grow under us. We'll look up the address in the car."

She followed him to his tan sedan and sat in the passenger seat. Before they exited her neighborhood, she'd accessed the county's property information system, found the address for Clinton and Maurine Vines, and plugged it into her GPS.

The clock read eight fifty-one when they pulled into the long driveway. "Just in the nick of time of arriving unfashionably late."

"You act like they're expecting us."

She shrugged. "Just something my parents drilled into me. 'Don't call or show up between nine and nine.'"

"Interesting."

They exited the car and arrived at the door simultaneously. She knocked. The soft padding of feet grew closer. A middle-aged woman with short, dark hair and perfect makeup opened the door.

"May I help you?"

"Mrs. Vines?" Suzanne asked.

She nodded.

"My name is Suzanne Marsh. I'm a private investigator. This is a Bart Oliver. We were wondering if we could ask you and Mr. Vines a few questions."

"About?"

Suzanne glanced at Bart. "Your son, Kingston."

Mrs. Vines crinkled her forehead. "Is he in trouble?"

"We're not sure."

She stepped back. "Sure. Come on in." She led them to a living room and sat on the edge of a straight-backed chair.

Suzanne and Bart sat on the matching sofa. Suzanne met the woman's gaze, recognizing the worry in them. "Is your husband available to meet with us, also?"

"Oh, I'm sorry. Clint hasn't been feeling well."

Suzanne glanced at Bart. "I'm sorry to hear that. A spring cold?"

"No." Mrs. Vines shook her head. "Some sort of stomach bug we think. He's been really weak and tired. It's almost like a flu, but he tested negative."

"You haven't gotten sick, though?"

"Well, I didn't feel good for a day or so, but never really got sick."

"How long's this been going on?" Suzanne asked. She wasn't sure why she continued to ask about Mr. Vines, but her gut told her the information was important.

"Off and on for about two weeks?"

"Off and on?"

Mrs. Vines nodded. "He was sick a few days, then started feeling better. He started eating again, then would feel bad again."

"That..."

"Yes?" Mrs. Vines asked.

"It just...reminds me of something. Is there anything he eats or drinks every day?"

"Not really." She tapped her perfectly manicured nails together. "Oh, well except coffee. He drinks it every day. Not the days he's thrown up, but every other day of his whole adult life."

"He by any chance use cream or sugar in his coffee?"

"Milk only."

"And you?" Suzanne leaned forward.

"I don't drink coffee. Have a glass of milk with a

cookie at bedtime once in a while. Why do you ask?"

"Just a hunch. It almost sounds like your husband is suffering from some type of food poisoning." Or just plain poisoning.

"I hadn't thought of that. Our milk didn't smell bad, but maybe." She stilled her hands and rested them in her lap. "You said you had some questions about Kingston."

"Yes, ma'am. We were wondering if he knew Mr. Jenkins."

"He did. What a tragedy, what happened. We are hoping Clint feels well enough to go to the funeral. He worked very closely with Tristan on all of our estate matters."

"By any chance, do you know if they were working on something recently."

Pink darkened Mrs. Vines cheeks. "They were."

"Would you be able to tell us what they were working on?"

She tapped her fingers on her knees. "I...I'm not sure Clint would want me to discuss that. It was a very private matter."

"Anything that might make Kingston upset."

"I-" She stood and strolled to the window.

"Mrs. Vines. It seems like you might know something about your husband and son. It might be upsetting, but we're concerned it might have something to do with

Tristan's murder. It sounds like you and your husband had a close relationship with him. If there is anything at all that you think might help us find out why he died so senselessly, we beg you to share it with us."

She continued to stare out of the window. "We were drafting a new will," her voice barely above a whisper as she spoke.

Suzanne met Bart's gaze. "Does Kingston know?"

She shook her head. "No. Clint and Tristan were meeting out of the office. He came here once, but mostly they met out of town."

"Does your son live here?"

She turned. "No. We kicked him out after he was arrested for drugs. We've tried to get him help for so long, but he refused to go to treatment after getting caught. We couldn't support him anymore. It broke our hearts, but with no change in sight, we can't take the risk he'll get our money if something happens to us. He'd blow it all. Instead, we've picked a charity to give fifty percent to."

"And the rest?" Suzanne asked.

"Kingston has a little girl who's four. She was born when he was a Junior in high school. We've set up a trust for her."

"So Kingston gets nothing?"

"Well, if we finish the will. I guess we'll have to work

with one of Tristan's partners now."

"It's not done yet?"

"No. Almost. Clint and I were supposed to meet with him on Monday to sign everything."

Suzanne stood and Bart followed. "I appreciate everything you've shared with us, Mrs. Vines. We're sorry for the loss of your friend. I didn't know Tristan very well, but from everything I've heard he was an amazing man."

"Thank you. He was."

Suzanne turned toward the front door. Mrs. Vines stood by it as they exited.

"Suzanne, right?"

She stopped and turned. "Yes."

"Do you really think Kingston could have had something to do with Tristan's death?"

"We're just turning over every stone. We don't have enough information to draw a clear conclusion." It was basically the truth. Although after the conversation they'd just had, Suzanne felt confident the pieces were fitting together perfectly.

Mrs. Vine nodded and closed the door.

CHAPTER 10

"WHAT'RE you thinking?" Burl asked once they were in the car.

"Kingston Vines somehow found out his parents were planning to write him out of their will."

He nodded as he cranked the car.

"I think he's trying to poison them, but it was taking too long. He couldn't shoot them because he'd be the first suspect. But taking out the lawyer, it would be less likely anyone would put it together. Especially if he knew Tristan was keeping the meetings off his books.

"I agree. Not sure about the poisoning, but the rest sounds plausible. How long until you call Tony?"

She sighed. "I'd love to find him first and bring him in."

He parked in her driveway, turned toward her, and rolled his eyes. "You're not a cop, Suzanne."

"I know that." She exited the car and headed to her

front door. She paused when she realized Bart's footsteps weren't following her. She turned. He stood by his door.

"It's late. I promised the kids I'd be home before ten tonight."

"Okay. Thanks for the evening."

"Don't do anything foolish."

She didn't answer.

"Promise me. Call Tony first thing in the morning."

"First thing."

"And you won't go looking for Kingston by yourself. Say it."

"I won't go looking for Kingston by myself."

He grinned. "Thanks. I'll touch base tomorrow."

Once in her house, she went through her bedtime routine. She walked to her bed, stared at it several heartbeats, then turned and strode to her office. Her mind raced with too much information to go to sleep any time soon.

The first search she did was for symptoms of poisoning. Browsing a page about cyanide poisoning, she mentally checked off the symptoms with what Mrs. Vines had told her. With the exceptions of a coma and seizures, it seemed to fit.

According to what she read, it was possible to put cyanide in a liquid. Even though the Vines had kicked Kingston out of the house, she'd place money on the fact that he still was able to access it. Even if they hadn't let him keep his key. He could have made a copy or had a way of sneaking in or out they didn't know about.

She printed off the page, then typed out the notes from her meeting with Mrs. Vines. Once finished, she added her theory.

It made sense. Kinston was a drug addict cut off from his parents' cash flow with the threat of losing his inheritance. If he came and went without them knowing, he could have easily overheard them talking about changing their will. Possibly, he could have even come by when Clint was meeting with Tristan. The boy would be desperate. Desperate people took dramatic actions, like killing the lawyer writing the will.

After writing everything out, she scanned the pages to make sure she hadn't forgotten anything. She debated emailing Tony before going to bed, but instead decided to wait until the morning.

She returned to her bedroom and sat on the edge of her bed. Tiredness refused to come. Maybe if she laid down.

She tried on her back, then on her side. Nothing helped. Finally, she reached for her phone and opened her reading app. She browsed her eBook options and picked a nonfiction book about the latest research in forensic science. She read until she couldn't hold her eyes open any longer.

Suzanne pried her eyes open and glanced at her clock. Almost eight. She needed to get moving. Her plan to meet Tony when his shift started flew out the window while she was still in dreamland, but she wouldn't be that far behind him. He should be in the office still. Most likely working on Tristan's case. Tediously going through the files they'd finally gotten from the lawyer's office.

After a shower, a small pot of coffee, and a couple of frozen waffles slathered in peanut butter, she printed the notes and grabbed her keys and headed out the door. Her car clock read eight forty.

She waved at the receptionist in the police station and marched to Tony's office. She knocked on his doorframe.

"Morning," he greeted her. A stack of folders littered his desk

"Mornin'. How's it going?"

"Monotonous."

"I bet."

He eyed the papers in her hand and sat back. "Find something?"

She grinned. "Maybe."

"Come in, Suzanne. Can I get you a coffee or something?"

She scrunched up her nose. "Police station coffee? No

thanks. I had the good stuff before I came."

"Well, you're here before noon, so it must be valuable."

She handed him her notes. He flipped through them, scanning each page. "You going to make me read all this?"

"I'm sure you can garner the main idea."

His eyes skimmed the last page. "Clinton Vines son? You really think he's capable of murder?"

She shrugged. "Money, or the danger of losing it, is a powerful motivator."

"True." He steepled his hands under his chin. "You went and talked with the Vines?"

She summarized her visit and search results.

"Cyanide poisoning? You really think so?"

"From what I read it's not that hard to come across. All Kingston needed was a way to get in without his folks knowing and inject the stuff in his parents' milk knowing his dad uses it in his coffee every day."

"I suppose..."

"He probably didn't count on how long it would take, or that his dad would quit drinking his coffee when he got so sick, allowing him a few days off the poison."

Tony nodded and rubbed his hands over his face. Several ticks of his wall clock filled the space before he replied. "Their own son trying to murder them."

She didn't respond.

"It's the most plausible theory we've come up with so far, though. Won't hurt to run by the Vines' house and suggest a trip to the hospital for testing." He met her gaze. "Don't suppose you know how to find Kingston Vines."

She told him about her visit to her friend Mike and the information she gathered from Dom.

"No address, though?"

"Nope."

"We couldn't get anything out of Slinger, either. But considering Kingston's connection with him, assuming he's the man called Princy, and the gun matching, I'd say that's enough to get a warrant."

"Thought it might be." She stood.

"Thanks, Suzanne."

"Of course."

He rose out of his chair. "Don't go looking for him."

She rolled her eyes. "Already heard that piece of advice from Bart."

Tony smiled. "Good man. You should listen to him."

"I'm not sure why men think a grown woman needs to be told what to do."

"Only stubborn women who put themselves in needless danger on a regular basis."

"It's part of the job description," she said.

"Not this time. It's not your job. Don't get me wrong, I appreciate everything you've done, but...."

"Got it, Tony. See you around."

She had two more hours before she was due on her job. Going back home to twiddle her thumbs wasn't an option. Research. It would help pass the time by and she would be keeping her word to Bart and Tony. They didn't say anything about her looking into Kingston Vines online.

She pulled into the downtown library's parking lot, grabbed her notebook and headed to the computers. The library was a great place to look into things when she didn't want a trail left on her phone or home computer.

First, she tackled social media. She found an account on two of the sites. It didn't look like he'd been on one in a while; his last post was almost two years ago. However, there was a great profile picture, plus a few photos friends had tagged him in.

She opened a blank document and copied and pasted the first picture to it. She grabbed two more since Kingston seemed to be fond of changing his hair. It was dark to almost black on one photo and bleached in another. At one time he kept it long, hanging over his ears and shirt collar. In another, he had it almost shaved. She printed the three sheets, grabbed her stuff and strolled to the printer. She deposited three dimes from her pocket and the printer whirred. She picked up the pictures and studied them. Just in case she ran across him, she told herself. She could also compare them to the picture in her car from Jamestown.

After grabbing a quick lunch at an Asian takeout restaurant, she turned toward her job location for the day. There was an extra car in the driveway. Suzanne parked across the street, a couple of spots down from where she'd parked the day before, but one where she still had a clear view of the living room. A second guy sat with her person of interest on the sofa. She picked up her camera and zoomed in. They each held an oversized joystick in their hands. Video games. She rolled her eyes.

She snapped a couple of pictures and picked up her lunch. She was halfway through her saucy noodles sprinkled with meat and veggies when her client jumped up. She threw the bucket on her dash without spilling it and grabbed her camera. By the time he and his buddy were finished high fiving each other, she'd snapped a dozen shots. She grinned. That was good enough. Not a single wince as he and bum number two congratulated each other on a hard-fought virtual win.

She'd stay long enough to finish her lunch. See if there were any more opportunities for her latest case to prove himself not injured.

CHAPTER 11

SUZANNE studied each picture, memorizing the details of Kingston Vines' face. He was an attractive kid. Pale blue eyes like his mother. Round face must have come from his father. In one picture, he looked too young to cause trouble, but she remembered that a lot could change in two years, especially for a teenager.

When comparing them to the picture from the crime scene, she determined the build was definitely the same. And when his hair was longer, it did have a curl to it.

Was this kid really capable of murder? Especially of plotting out the painful, long-coming death of his own parents? She shook her head. She'd always known she was blessed with great parents and not everyone was. The Vines seemed like good, normal people, but she'd also learned in her life and career that one never knew what went on behind the closed doors of someone else's house.

She glanced at her client every few minutes, but he and his buddy hadn't moved much from their crouched positions on the sofa. Must be an intense game. She had enough to report back to the insurance company. She also had another job she'd planned to start the next day. Wouldn't hurt to check the woman out a day early.

Her mind ached to go find Kingston. If he hung around East River, she could most likely come up with whatever hole he crawled into to sleep every night.

But she'd promised. As stubborn as she was, she was a woman who kept her word. She wouldn't go looking for him.

She reached into her back seat and pulled the file she had studied the day before after receiving it. A mom, forty, pulled her back out at her job as a therapist. She was going to therapy herself, but the company hadn't done any scans yet. Too expensive, the insurance company said. In her opinion, doing an x-ray or CT scan from the beginning would save them a lot of hassle in fighting legit claims. Of course, then Suzanne would have less work. She liked a steady paycheck.

She put the address in her phone and cranked the engine. She'd scope out what she could for an hour or so. And check in with Tony once she arrived.

After parking, Suzanne pulled her phone out. *Any*

updates?

Her phone buzzed a couple minutes later. *Vines at the hospital. Running tests.*

She replied with a thumb's up. Guess they'd know soon if at least part of her theory was right.

She didn't see any movement in the house. No large picture window on the front of this one. She'd have to hover and wait for the client to come outside or go somewhere.

Her phone vibrated.

Positive. Starting antidote and oxygen.

Suzanne had never felt worse about being right. Kingston was poisoning his own parents. If he was capable of that, he'd have no qualms about gunning down a man he barely knew.

Glancing at the quiet house once more, she decided this case could wait one more day. It would probably take several, anyway.

With nothing else productive to do, well except the paperwork she'd need to fill out when she got home, she decided to drive by the Vines' house. Just to review everything she knew with a visual connected to the case.

On the way, she stopped by a gas station, filled up, and tossed the trash from her car. It might be her second office, but she'd rather it didn't look like she lived in it.

She always fussed at Mark and how he never cleaned out his car. He kept receipts, napkins, tools, and anything else he'd ever taken in it. She'd have given anything right after he died to have his mess back. Brianna and Brendan had to clean his car out when it came time for her to sell it. She couldn't bear clearing out his mess.

Suzanne reduced her speed as she passed the Vines' house, turned around in the cul-de-sac, and parked across the street. She began with everything she knew about Tristan's shooting, turning each detail over in her mind, examining each bit of information from every angle.

A movement on the right side of the house caught her attention. Someone disappeared behind the Vines' house. She grabbed her cell, closed her car door behind her quietly, and dashed across the street.

A path of steppingstones lined the side of the house to a door leading into the garage. She tiptoed down it and onto the grass. Pausing at the corner, she glanced around it. The same figure, dressed in ratty jeans and a dark blue hoody, entered a window. She couldn't see his face, but his build matched Kingston's.

She crept along the back wall and peaked in the window. A bedroom decorated in black and red. Very masculine. Of course. He could have left his bedroom window unlocked when he was kicked out. Who would think to go around and check to make sure all the windows were locked? She never did.

For half a second, she debated going in after him. Knowing Tony, though, he wouldn't hesitate charging her with breaking and entering to prove a point.

Instead, she snuck around the house, peaking in the windows. She stopped at the third one. The kitchen. The man stood with the refrigerator door open, his back to her. He pulled something out of his pocket. She lifted her phone and snapped several pictures.

"Move, just a bit. Let me see exactly what you're doing," she whispered.

As if he heard her, he twisted slightly as he squeezed a syringe into the milk carton. Next, he repeated the action into an apple juice container. She hit the button to take photos in rapid fire.

He closed the refrigerator and turned. Suzanno ducked, praying he hadn't seen her.

She had everything she needed and continued around the side of the house she was on, keeping low. She froze at the feel of cold metal on her neck.

"Some em' I can help you with?"

She straightened out and turned her head. Ice blue eyes met her gaze. "I came by to check on Maurine. I'd been by yesterday and was worried about her."

He narrowed his eyes. "Couldn't knock on the front

door like normal peeps?"

"Saw someone go around back. Thought there might be a burglar."

A grin turned up the corners of his lips, but didn't reach his eyes. "I ain't no burglar."

"Okay, great." She stepped back. "Then we're good. I'll catch Maurine later."

He grabbed her arm and pressed the knife back to her throat. "Not so fast. What else did you see?"

"Nothing." Her phone vibrated.

His eyes darted to her hand. "Anyone know you're here?"

"Yes, my partner."

He studied her. "You a cop?"

"Ha! No."

"You said partner."

She swallowed the bile working its way up her throat. "He's my um, we work together."

"But you're not five-o?"

"Not on your life."

"You're awful snoopy for not a cop. What do you do?"

"Work in insurance." It was technically the truth.

His eyes narrowed to slits.

Her phone buzzed again.

"Someone determined to get you."

She stopped herself from shrugging, not wanting the sharp blade pushed further into her skin. "Just work stuff, I'm sure. We done here yet?"

"Don't think so. Might as well have some fun first." He sneered at her and pulled her to the back of the house.

"What are you doing?"

"Don't trust you. You're coming with me."

His grip on her arm was surprisingly tight given his lack of bulk. Her phone buzzed again and she took a chance by glancing at it. Tony had left her three messages. From what she could make out, they were on their way to test items in the house for cyanide. His last text demanded she respond.

Kingston stopped by the window she'd seen him climb in. He released her arm, but kept the blade at her neck. At that moment she wished she didn't know how quickly he could slice through her carotid artery and how fast her life would drain away if he did. Quicker than Tony could arrive, find her, and stop the bleeding.

He shoved the window up. "Climb in."

She had the advantage now. He'd have to back off with the knife when she climbed in.

She slipped her phone in her back pocket, hoisted herself up, and rolled onto the floor. He huffed behind her and she took off, twisting the lock on the door before pulling it closed. The lock was on the inside, but it might buy her an extra couple of seconds while he opened it.

"Get back here," he yelled.

She turned left down the hallway and took an almost immediate right. The front door was straight ahead. His footsteps pounded behind her. She raced to the door and turned the deadbolt and lock on the handle.

He grabbed her hair and yanked her back. "Not as fast or smart as you think. I said we're going to have fun."

"No," she screamed at the top of her lungs. "Kingston don't."

He stopped, glaring at her. "How do you know my name?"

"I told you, I know your mother."

"She wouldn't have talked about me. She never talks about me to her friends."

Suzanne didn't know what to respond to that.

Banging on the door made them both jump.

"Police! Open up."

Tony. He made it.

Kingston's eyes widened.

"You haven't done anything." She touched her neck. "Not even a nick. It's your parents' house, so you're good. Just let them in."

He shook his head. "No way."

"The house is surrounded, Kingston. Your parents gave us a key. We don't even have to use force to get in."

He pulled her close, returning the blade to the soft part of her skin a couple inches below her ear. "I have a hostage."

"You'll never make it. They have guns."

"Says the woman with the knife to her neck. They always protect the hostage. Always."

He turned her to face away from him and wrapped his arm around her, moving the knife to the other side of her neck. "Open the door," he demanded.

She did and met Tony's gaze. Another officer stood to his left.

"Stay back or the woman bites it," Kingston said.

She blinked once. Then twice rapidly. On her third blink in the third set, Suzanne dropped down, the knife scraping her chin, and Tony pounced forward. He grabbed Kinston's knife-wielding wrist and twisted it behind his back with one hand and pointed his pistol at him with the other. Suzanne rolled out of the way as the second officer relieved Kinston of his weapon. A third officer rounded the house, scanned the scene and rushed to her side.

"You okay, ma'am?" He pressed a hand to her neck.

"Just a nick."

An ambulance siren sounded in the distance. Great. They'd want to assess the damage.

The officer helped her stand. "Let's at least get a rag

on that."

She looked down. The scrape was making a mess of her blouse. She followed him to the police car parked on the curb. He pulled a rag out and handed it to her.

"Thanks."

The siren grew louder, then the flashing lights rounded the corner and headed toward them.

Tony was going through his 'you have the right' spiel while leading Kingston to the car. The boy scowled and shot her daggers. The officer next to her moved her away, gently leading her by the elbow to Tony's unmarked vehicle.

The ambulance pulled up and the EMT's hopped out. Glancing around, she saw several curious neighbors standing on their front stoops and driveways. Just one reason she preferred her job to being a cop. No lights and sirens. No unwarranted attention.

"You all right, ma'am?"

"I'm fine. Just a small cut."

"Mind if we look at it."

She followed him to the ambulance and removed the rag. He pulled out a bottle with liquid in it and another piece of cloth. "This might sting a bit, but it'll help disinfect the wound and let us get a clearer view of the damage."

She winced as he completed his job.

"Well, no stitches necessary. A Band-Aid should do. Shall I?" He asked when done.

"If you have one, I can take care of it."

He handed her a small one and she stuck it on. Tony strolled over and raised an eyebrow at her.

"What? I didn't go looking for him."

"You just happened to find him."

"I came by to sit in front of the house while processing all the information. I do that sometimes. Too familiar of a setting can stifle my mind."

"Uh huh." He sounded skeptical.

"I was sitting out front when I saw someone dart between the houses."

"Ever think about letting me in on your little venture?"

"I was about to text you what I saw when—"

"When you found yourself in the hands of a suspected murderer?"

"Yeah, that," she answered.

"Glad you're okay."

"Thanks. Me, too. Oh." She pulled her phone out of her pocket. "Got some pictures you might be interested in."

"Yeah?"

She nodded. "Also, I think checking the milk and apple juice cartons would be a great place to start."

He shook his head. "You just can't help yourself, can you?"

She smiled. "It's in my blood."

CHAPTER 12

A HAND rested on Suzanne's arm. She stopped and turned.

"Mrs. Marsh, I wanted to thank you."

Suzanne took the hand Lenora Jenkins held out to her. "I, um, you're welcome."

The woman's eyes were bloodshot, but she offered a small smile. "Detective Henderson tells me you were at Jamestown when my husband was killed and were a bit relentless in helping find the man responsible, even though it wasn't your job."

Suzanne wondered what Tony's tone had been when he'd said the last bit. She shrugged. "It's the investigator in me. Just can't leave a mystery alone."

"Well, whatever it was, I appreciate everything you did. My Tristan was an amazing man." She paused and swallowed, her eyes filling. "To know there is some justice for his death is a comfort, as small as it may be."

"Of course."

Mrs. Jenkins glanced back. "I guess I better go back in."

Suzanne nodded, exhaled, and pushed through the door. She hit the unlock button on her key fob.

"Suzanne," a familiar voice called.

She swiveled. "Hey, Bart."

"Leaving already?"

"You know I don't do funerals. Visitation is bad enough."

He drew closer. "I'm sure it's still hard."

She met his gaze, but didn't reply.

He leaned against the car and she joined him. "You did good work. Right up until the point you had a knife held to your throat."

"I kept my word. I didn't go looking for him."

"But when you found him, did you let anyone know?"

"Instinct. I didn't exactly have time to think."

"Take a breath next time. We like having you around."

She saluted him and he chuckled.

"Guess I owe you that dinner at the Boathouse."

"Yes, you do."

"Pick a couple dates and I'll check my calendar and the kids' schedules."

"Okay," she replied.

"You know, we never finished that last game of cards."

"No, we didn't. I'd love to finish it. I'm feeling much luckier today."

He laughed. "Maybe you used all your luck in preserving your life."

She grinned. "Perhaps."

"Or maybe luck didn't have anything to do with it."

She turned to meet his gaze.

"You know how I feel about luck," he said.

"I do." She tore her eyes away and stared at the wispy clouds blowing across the sky. "And you know how I feel about that topic."

"One day, on the right day, you'll be ready and I'll be here." He reached over and covered her hand with his.

"I know you will." She squeezed his hand, then pulled away. "I'm going to go back to my new job for a couple hours. You staying for the funeral and food and all that?"

"Yeah. How about I come over after picking up the kids? We'll force them into doubles."

"Sammy will love that."

"I know, but it's good for them."

"All right, I'll see you in a few."

Suzanne drove to her newest job. So far, the woman seemed like a legitimate case. Only time would tell for sure, though.

Thank you so much for taking the time to read this little book! Living in the Historic Triangle, where our country's roots are strong and deep, is a great privilege. This is why I enjoy so writing books set here. I hope that this story, the first of what will hopefully be many with Suzanne Marsh, entertained you and blessed you.

I want to thank the Lord for answering my prayers for divine writing inspiration after a long dry spell. It is difficult for a writer to lack energy, motivation, and ideas to put a story on paper. But I learned a ton about building a house and taking sabbatical during that time. God was faithful in the times of struggle just as much as He is in the times of success.

I also want to thank my husband for his continuous patience when dinner doesn't get cooked and the floor doesn't get swept when I am on a writing role. And for dragging me away from the computer for quality family time on a regular basis.

I want to express deep gratitude for my children and their understanding with Mommy's hobby and help to keep our house somewhat close to order.

I want to also thank the countless talented authors that I read on a regular basis. You inspire me to be a better writer and add quality stories to the field of books.

I'd love for you to check out my other books, which you can find at Amazon or on my website. My goal is to write books for the whole family, so you will find picture books, a young adult novel, women's fiction, nonfiction, and Bible studies. I'd also be blessed to hear from you! Feel free to email me at tracy_wainwright@yahoo.com.

Sincerely,

Tracy Wainwright

Other books by Tracy Wainwright

Fiction

In an Instant

Her Whole Self

Riding the Wind

Nonfiction

A Transformed Mind

A Transformed Mouth

A Transformed Ministry

Living Stress Free

Picture Books

Apple vs. Asparagus

Counting from Creation

Activity Books

Apple vs. Asparagus Christmas Activity Book

Apple vs. Asparagus Coloring Book

Made in the USA
Middletown, DE
03 May 2024

53802620R00057